I Love Blue Macaroons

By: Matthew L. Smith

Illustrated By: Courtney McNamara

For Jarred & Emma

What I wouldn't do for a blue macaroon…

I would jump to the sky
and leap over the moon.

I would fly to Paris
in a hot air balloon.

I would go to the jungle

and swing with baboons.

I would ride on a bus
with a pack of raccoons.

I would crow with a rooster
in the late afternoon.

I would build a snowman
in the month of June.

I would even eat one
with a spoon.

I love blue macaroons!

60431100R00015

Made in the USA
Columbia, SC
14 June 2019